THE PRECIOUS TRIO

THREE KIDS ADVENTUROUS STORY

JAHANVI TRIVEDI

I would like to dedicate this book to all the kids and young readers who like to read good stories in the world full of internet contents.

I would like to dedicate the book to all who inspired and encouraged me to write stories for kids.

Contents

Preface

Thanks for choosing this book. The book is a story of three kids solving a mystery. It will drive you through the jungle, dense yet beautiful. The childlike experiences and experiments of the kids will get you to your own memory lane.

I thank my family, friends and my daughter Aadhya Trivedi who had inspired me to write a story considering children.

You can give feedback, comments and reach out to me at modha_jahanvi@rediffmail.com.

Happy reading!!

Acknowledgements

My acknowledgements goes for my parents, husband, my daughter Aadhya. Special thanks to my nephew Kush Modha who has taken out his valuable time from studies to contribute for the beautiful pictures of the book.

Thanks to Almighty God for inspiring me to write and put down my thoughts on a paper.

Prologue

Three children of age around 11 to 12 years old are roaming between 100-150 feet tall trees and green weeds perhaps searching for something.

"The trees are sooo tall that your elder brother cannot reach even lowest branch!" Said the eldest child named Raghu who is 12 to Krina who is 11.

"Why? Is my brother a monkey who always keep jumping?" answered Krina.

"No, in fact Raghu's brother need jumping practice daily these days as he has got job in Royal Circus as a monkey!" laughed the third one who is Lucky, again ageing 11 years.

The 3 naughtiest children of the school, have lost here at 3 p.m. on a winter afternoon of 15th December 2019, in a not so dangerous but dense jungle near a resort.

CHAPTER ONE

The unknown girl

Three children of age around 11 to 12 years old are roaming between 100-150 feet tall trees and green weeds perhaps searching for something.

"The trees are sooo tall that your elder brother cannot reach even lowest branch!" Said the eldest child named Raghu who is 12 to Krina who is 11.

"Why? Is my brother a monkey who always keep jumping?" answered Krina.

"No, in fact Raghu's brother need jumping practice daily these days as he has got job in Royal Circus as a monkey!" laughed the third one who is Lucky, again ageing 11 years.

The 3 naughtiest children of the school, have lost here at 3 p.m. on a winter afternoon of 15th December 2019, in a not so dangerous but dense jungle near a resort.

"All thanks to your stupid idea of exploring the jungle" said Krina to Raghu.

"But you had also agreed to come with us. You girls are always spoilsports!" replied Lucky making faces to Krina.

"No, I am not the spoilsport, but I am the bravest of all three of us" Krina was spontaneous in answering. "anybody home, anybody home, anybody home?" she shouted so loud that echo effect in this lonely jungle was thrice instead of twice.

"Guys, please don't fight. Lets find the way to resort", said Raghu always thinking himself as if he is the only grown up kid among three of them. But krina and Lucky are still busy cracking jokes and doing mischief. Lucky was showing Krina how Raghu's brother must be jumping all the time for job practice!!

Suddenly a sweet voice said, "Hi". A very soft sound got heard from behind just like whispering of a girl. The 3 children turned to the direction of sound. They got scared at once. Ghost!

But they got relaxed as they saw a normal city girl aged about 22 to 23 years, dressed in casual pink colored plain T-Shirt and blue Jeans. Her hair were long but neatly combed and tied in a ponytail. She was not wearing any makeup still she looked charming. She was not a very beautiful woman but an average looking girl.

Children found one more victim for a mischievous prank. The 3 children built up a quick plan.

"Didi, did you clear your geography subject in grade 5?" asked Krina

"Yes of course, but why are you asking me this question?" said Didi.

"Then you must be knowing the way out of this jungle" this time it was Lucky.

"This jungle was not there in my syllabus" Didi was also smart.

"Then how will you go out of this jungle?" asked Raghu thinking he is more smart then Didi.

"Hmm, good question. I will not go anywhere because I stay here." Googly ball! Raghu had heard of this word in cricket but googly dialogue? Now what? This girl is the only hope and help to find their way to resort.

Few days ago:

Its 1st December and one of the most pleasant winter has just started in the city of Mumbai. Who says winters are not there in Mumbai? Its very much there in its mini form, for fifteen days. And people live their whole season in these few days. This winter also, people all over the city were ready to welcome the season. Most of the city locals enjoy small or big picnics to nearby locations or faraway place. The Christmas vacation is a time when almost all nearby tourist places, picnic spots, hotels and resorts remain occupied because of the pleasant winter season.

How can the schools and colleges remain behind when the entire city is enjoying picnics? Sir Joseph school of Mumbai, decided to plan a picnic too.

The class 6th children of Sir Joseph School were very excited today as teacher announced a picnic to the nearby resort "Suhana resort" for 1 day.

As soon as the announcement was made, the 3 children Raghu, Krina and Lucky started jumping in the class. Teacher could not control this noise and left the classroom. The 3 children started discussing their plans about the picnic.

"I will take my cricket kit and we will play cricket" said Raghu.

"No I will carry badminton kit and we will play badminton there." Krina said.

"You must take a doll with you!" suggested Raghu to Krina.

"Oh, you want to play with dolls?" asked Krina. "Sure, I will take one for you, don't worry."

Lucky did not have any preference as such but he preferred to support Krina as she was the youngest of all. "I will play badminton with Krina while Raghu will play with Krina's doll." Giggled Lucky.

"And yes, my protective mom will definitely pack my sweater, dark glasses, 3 caps, 4 handkerchiefs, 5 tissues," said Lucky. "All you guys will not need to carry any of these stuff. We will share."

"But Mam said, there is a swimming pool and we need to carry swimming suit and an extra pair of clothes, I don't think we will get any time to play any games. We can enjoy swimming whole day!" said Raghu and the children finally agreed to carry the stuff used for swimming and some extra safety things that everyone's mom will pack.

The children were best friends since their diaper and milk bottle days as they were from the same residential society "Shivdham society". They had taken admission in the same school. Today their friendship has grown much closer and stronger with their age. They had named their group as "Precious Trio". And their parents had given them a name "Naughty trio". All 3 children's parents had equally good relations with each other. These relations helped the kids in all their activities, which they do jointly. Be it any game, sport, contest or picnic. So today, it was a unanimous "yes" from parents for the picnic.

The Precious Trio discussed for 15 continuous days about the picnic whenever and wherever they met. The picnic was scheduled on 15th December, the birthday of Krina too.

"I will carry a bag of chocolates for distribution", said Krina while playing cricket in the society playground with the group.

"A bag will not be enough for Raghu. Krina, you will need to carry a box full of 5 bags for this chocolate boy." Said Lucky teasing Raghu.

No, I don't think that's a good idea, you can distribute sweets in the class itself, as there will be lots of children who may not join the picnic. They will miss your sweets" Raghu, the mature boy said ignoring Lucky's jokes, which he usually does. Moreover, the children were also taught importance of equality in the class so Krina happily accepted the suggestion of Raghu.

Then, finally after a long wait, the previous night of the big day arrived! The Precious trio became extremely busy in packing the stuff that they wanted to carry to the picnic. Their moms had 100 of instructions to give but who listens!

"Don't go far away in the forest", Krina's mom had said that night but she didn't care.

"Always be with your teachers and friends", Raghu's mom had said this but Raghu is busy in packing his swimming suit and other board games which can be played if time permits.

Lucky's mom wrote a note of instructions and put inside his bag because she knew that her child is neither in the mood of listening to any of her instructions nor will he remember any of them.

Finally, the kids went for sleeping but who sleeps on the previous night of the exciting day? None of them was able to sleep. In fact no child of that class was sleeping that night. There was utmost excitement in their minds for the next day picnic. 100s of plans and 100s of activities to do. Which child in the world remains calm on such occasions? Do grown-ups remain calm on previous night of the exciting day ahead?

CHAPTER TWO

The happy day:

Next day morning, i.e. December 15, the Precious trio woke up much earlier than the scheduled time in the morning and they woke up their parents too!

Usually, the moms or dads wake up their children for the school and kids give 1000s of excuses for not waking up. "Today not feeling well, or yesterday night I slept late, etc." are their favorite ones. In fact one fine day mischievous Krina had given an excuse that, "today teacher will remain absent so I will go late!" And her Mom poured a full glass of water on her face hearing this extremely weird excuse.

But, today it was a role reversal for the families. All the activities of getting ready for the picnic got finished in the blink of an eye. Brushing of teeth, bathing, breakfast, milk, combing hair, wearing uniform, carrying Identity cards, everything checked by the kids themselves. Wow, the mothers wished the children could be equally responsible and active on the days of regular school. Anyways, today is the big day for children so they did not initiate any of the instructive or advisory talks.

The Precious trio as they have named their group reached on time to the school sharp at 7.45 a.m. The picnic bus was ready and supposed to depart at 8.30 after all the children arrive. The teachers gave 100 instructions, paired and grouped the children with each other so that they don't get lost, distributed snack boxes to be eaten during the travel, took attendance and finally they all said the prayers and left for the picnic. The noise, oh sorry, the journey begins.

Lots of excitement was there in the 2 buses. Today nobody could stop children or even teachers from making noise. Activities like singing of songs, dancing of kids, teasing of friends and many verbal games were going on. Krina gave one doll to Raghu that she had actually carried with her! Raghu was about to throw away the dolls but teacher stopped him. The 3 kids were best friends but smarter then each other in teasing each other.

Within 2 hours the buses arrived at the picnic spot. Wow, what a lovely resort it was!

A big ground and a big swimming pool especially for kids were the most attractive pieces of this resort. They were looking as if they were waiting only for the kids to come over and have a splash! The school was greeted with a welcome drink-watermelon juice and then children were taken immediately to the kid's swimming pool without wasting any further time. The pool was hardly 3-4 feet deep so that kids can enjoy the water sufficiently but do not have danger of being drowned. The resort management has also kept one lifeguard who was constantly watching the kids.

The children jumped sprinkled water on each other, swam and did hundreds of such acts. Some children caught cough but the fun continued.

"Sometimes I just wish I never grow up, childhood life is so exciting", Sarika Mam, Maths teacher was discussing with Sneha Mam, English teacher.

"Yes, I wish too! No care about what will happen tomorrow. And most importantly the children are so innocent that they rely blindly on anyone. Sometimes I feel that being extremely innocent is also harmful," said Sneha Mam.

After the 3 hours of fun filled swimming pool games, the children were feeling extremely hungry. The resort staff was at their service. Delicious and mouthwatering lunch got served. All items were favorite of children. Today no elder would stop them from eating pizza, pasta, burger, sandwiches, chocolates cakes and pastry. They could eat as much as they want. The Precious trio ate as if they had not eaten for days!! The trio discussed a plan of further activities during lunchtime itself.

Soon lunchtime got over and teacher allowed the children to freely explore the resort. But, on one condition, they had to remain in groups and return in 1 hour.

Now it's the time to execute the plan that was made while eating pizza. The Precious trio moved towards the cricket ground of the resort as Raghu was fond of cricket. But, the ground was not active, due to extended monsoon, which had recently got over. There were plenty of unwanted weeds grown in the ground, which were yet to be cleaned. Due to these weeds there were lot of dangerous insects in the weeds. Some insects were looking like small size monsters! Krina got one insect bite and started crying as loud as possible.

"Usual girly tantrums!" said Raghu.

"No, I am strong." Said Krina and the Trio went ahead of the cricket ground. Soon they got between big groups of tall trees.

There was a mini jungle nearby to the resort. The beauty of the jungle was truly an art of the Almighty God. The children had never seen such a beauty of the nature in Mumbai.

Between the tall trees there was small cute spring with icy cold water. The water drops were looking like freshly cut diamonds. Each diamond was worth 10 million bucks. Beside the spring, there was small lake wherein some beautiful lotuses were just about to say "Hi" to the kids. Though the trees, weeds, plants and entire jungle were very much unknown to the kids, yet, the kids felt like each part of the jungle was calling them and wanted to play with them. No artificial thing would match the nature beauty created by God. The kids wanted to explore more and more so they went ahead and ahead into the jungle.

After an hour of walking, Krina said, "I am now tired of walking, I want to return."

"See, now who is getting weaker? The strong person of our team Ms. Krina says she is tired!" Raghu made 10 different faces while completing these 2 sentences. But Lucky also got tired. So this time also he supported Krina.

"Ok, so now we don't have any option of going further. The two brave soldiers of our team are not ready to explore more. Now its turn to return to the resort." Finally, Raghu agreed.

"But where is the way?" Lucky asked.

"I know, let's go reverse and we will reach the resort", said Raghu thinking himself most mature person of the team.

The children took a U-turn and started walking. They walked for further half an hour but could not find any sight of the resort. Very soon, they realized that they have got lost in the jungle.

While they were blaming and teasing each other, suddenly a very sweet but silent voice said to their ears "Hi". The children saw the city girl in pink top in front of them.

After taking funny exam of the girl, Raghu sincerely said, "Didi, we have lost in this jungle. Do you know the way to "Suhana resort?"

"Yes, of course. God has sent me to help you guys. I know every way to any place".

"But you just said, I don't go anywhere and this jungle map was not there in your syllabus!" asked clever Krina.

"I was kidding with 3 little kids, hahaha!" Laughed the girl.

"Are you a Google map?" asked Lucky with a teasing tone.

"Yes, follow me" said the girl and started walking in an opposite direction.

After a further 30 minutes silent walk, the girl led the group to a big and tallest tree of the jungle.

There she turned to the kids and said, "I think I have also lost the way to resort".

"Oh no, are you mad? Sometimes saying you do not know the way, then leading us to this unknown path saying you know the way and now you are saying, you have lost the way. How will we reach the resort?" Asked Krina.

"Don't worry little girl" the unknown girl said.

Mom had said not to rely on unknown people, thought Krina, now all 3 of us have relied on a half mad girl. However, she did not have courage to speak.

"What is your name Didi?" Raghu somehow gathered courage and asked.

"See my Identity card, I am from Sir Joseph School" the girl showed her teacher ID card. The kids just jumped out in joy on knowing that the Didi was one of the teachers of their school.

"My name is Aarti. Now are you convinced that I am not an unknown person?" the kids just laughed and laughed until they fall down.

But now, the evening was getting darker and the kids were just worried about how to reach the resort.

Here in resort, the teachers, resort staff and management got extremely scared and worried on knowing about 3 missing kids. The resort manager had sent one of his experienced staff member along with one teacher of the school in search of the three kids. It was time to leave for the school but the teachers could not start their return journey without taking the missing kids. They immediately informed the principle in Mumbai.

"The parents will start arriving from 5 p.m. onwards to receive their kids. And at 4.45 p.m. you have not even started your journey?" Scolded the principle Mam to the teachers. Ultimately, after 15 minutes of arguments teachers finally started their journey back to school leaving one of their teachers with the resort staff to continue the search of the missing kids.

"The parents are not going to leave us. Tomorrow's newspaper will have a big headline about our missing kids" Sneha Mam said.

"Don't worry, our teacher and resort staff will soon find out the missing kids and return back", said Sarika Mam, however deep inside she was also equally worried. Moreover, the teachers were worried for losing their jobs for being so careless. This was the first time in the history of the school that a happy event like a picnic turned into a tensed and sad event. The bus returned but there was no joy in the air. The remaining children also sensed the worry- some faces of their teachers. No one dared to speak anything on the return journey.

Back in the school that evening after releasing remaining kids Sneha Mam, Sarika Mam, Principle Mam and the parents of Precious Trio had an elaborated meeting. The parents did not have any option but to complaint to police and tell the media about the carelessness. The principle Mam consoled them and guaranteed them that their left over staff will find the kids and return soon.

The meeting got over after 2 hours but no one was convinced. Thoughts of worry and tensions had occupied the space in the minds of the parents.

Raghu's father even decided to go to the resort and search for the kids on his own, but Lucky's father said, "If the resort staff is searching the kids then I am sure he will find them successfully and we will have our kids".

Sneha and Sarika, two very responsible and knowledgeable teachers of the school spent that night sleepless only ready to welcome tomorrow's newspaper with headline of their missing kids.

CHAPTER THREE

The Sunday:

Next day morning was a Sunday, which is otherwise supposed to be a relaxed and fun day in everybody's life, is not a day at all today. It was all dark everywhere. Where is the sunrise today, there are only dark clouds in the sky!

Sarika Mam took today's newspaper without even bothering about brushing her teeth. She usually had a habit of reading newspaper with a cup of masala chai. But today she didn't have any time to prepare masala chai. She started searching for the news of her school. She turned and turned the pages. There was no headline about Sir Joseph School. There was neither a single small news of her school. May be parents of the kids are extremely kind for not telling to media about their missing children.

"Ring", the landline phone rang. "Hey, Sarika, the kids have returned to their homes!" Sneha Mam had called up.

"Actually they had returned yesterday night only, I tried your number several times but your phone was not reachable." Then I tried your landline but it was coming as line faulty. Sarika immediately realized that her mobile phone battery was not charged. She forgot to charge her phone in the tension of the missing kids.

The cloud had just got cleared from the sky and a beautiful sunrise is visible now. Sarika never felt so relaxed in her life before. She immediately put her phone on charging and cleaned her teeth as she usually taught her students about personal hygiene. Made a hot cup of masala tea and sat with her newspaper and teacup in the balcony. Sunday is after all a fun day. Now let the fun begin.

In the joy and relaxation of receiving the kids that night, everyone forgot to ask the kids what had happened in the picnic with them.

Back to Jungle:

After showing her identity card and revealing her name, Aarti Sahani gave her full background knowledge to the kids.

"I am the daughter of builder Sahani group. My father wanted to become the owner of this resort few years back. Actually, I am right now a dead person. If you are interested in knowing my history further I will tell you, otherwise if you feel bored, then also I will not stop. Because its only me who knows the way to resort. You have no choice but to remain with me as much as I want."

The girl spoke in one breath. The kids felt an extremely cold wave in the middle of the afternoon inside their veins, almost about to faint. But next moment, Krina laughed out loud.

"You mean, you are a ghost!"

"Yes".

"A ghost in Jeans and with identity card of our school?" Lucky said, giving a hi five to Krina.

"Just look at my ID card carefully. Its printed in year 2010. What is today's date?"

The trio got serious now. But immediately Raghu asked as if something just clicked in his mind, "how do we trust that you are real ghost? You might be wearing an old ID card intentionally to scare kids like us!"

"Ok, tell me what I should do to prove myself?" said Aarti, thinking that the kids are over smart but after all they are kids so they might not be too demanding.

"You need to sing a melodious song.. just like Ghumnaam hai koi...!" demanded Krina. She is fond of music.

"Ok." Clearing her throat, Aarti started, "Gumnaam hai ....koi, Badnaam hai....koi"

"You think this is melodious? Thank god this jungle doesn't have dogs, otherwise they will accompany you. Stop this. Now sing, Aayega.... Aayega..... aayega...." Said Lucky, as if demanding song on a music show.

"I don't know more songs. And what do you think, am I hosting an on demand musical performance or what? That too free of cost! And how do you know about these old melodies, which even I don't know!" now Aarti tried to become an angry young woman but all efforts wasted. The kids are not so serious.

"Simple, google on old hindi melodies." Krina was quick to answer.

Finally Aarti said only one thing, "dig here little deep and you will find my dead body" This statement finally made the kids believe that Aarti is a ghost, though not so scary!

Now they thought, "We have encountered a real ghost! A real live ghost! No, a real dead ghost! No, a dead person!" Still confused what words to use. Until now, they had listened to the stories of ghosts but now its time to experience the real thrill. They were trapped in the hands of this girl. Should they faint now? Feel nervous? Strokes of low BP, high BP or direct heart attack? But nothing like that happened to any of the kids. After all they were brave kids and had named themselves Precious trio. It's time to prove their name right now.

Finally Aarti continued on telling her story. All of them had no choice but to listen carefully.

CHAPTER FOUR

The story of Aarti:

"My father is a builder as I said earlier. He used to purchase old properties and build new buildings."

"Back in 2010, the place where the resort is built now was a palace of an old king Vijaysingh since 1919. The king was no more living and his great grandchildren had settled in London. The entire palace was an empty useless place. One fine morning, my father read in the newspaper that the king's great grandson Suraj Singh wanted to sell his palace.

"Because the palace was haunted!" giggled Lucky, "wow, thrilling story!"

"Keep your jokes with you, Lucky. Lets listen to Didi." Raghu always tried to make efforts of acting mature.

These kids are not going to fear. Thought Aarti.

"Shut up", said Aarti. "There is no other ghost other then me. Okay. So, lets continue. Prince had invited the interested buyers and was coming to Mumbai to crack the deal. My father immediately called up the number given in the newspaper ad and showed his interest in buying the property."

"Great" Prince Suraj Singh had said. The meeting got fixed for the next week and visit to the palace was decided. After the visit, my father was so impressed with the palace that he lent the token money to Prince as a booking of the deal."

Again coming week, my father showed the desire to visit the palace. The prince had to agree.

"You also come along. In future you will have to manage our business," my father wanted me, a 20 year old girl, to accompany him.

Actually, my father had always wanted me to become a businesswoman and I was also equally interested so without wasting a single moment, I got ready to accompany my father."

"You know kids, just like you could not sleep the yesterday night in the excitement of today's picnic, I also could not sleep that previous night in the excitement of visiting a real palace."

Until now I had only read in my history subject about palace, but that day I was going to get the opportunity to visit a real palace!"

"How do you know that we could not sleep yesterday night?" asked Lucky.

"Its so obvious. Because of lots of thoughts and excitement in the mind, one cannot sleep peacefully. And kids are most excited about such picnics and happy events. Don't forget I am, sorry I was a teacher in your school for 1 year. I was teaching Maths to class 7th students of your school. Children were my best friends. I can read little bit of children psychology. After school, I used to play with them, ask them maths puzzle! I was their favorite maths teacher, they always told me. I remember how much my students used to love me. Just sharing one incident. There was an interschool Maths quiz on the day of my birthday. My students and I had prepared very well for the competition. But, because of extreme pressure, I got a low BP stroke and fainted just during final round of the competition. When I woke up from the unconsciousness,

I received the news by my students that we had won the finals of the competition and they brought me a winning trophy! The best birthday gift of my life. I remember everything about my school life as a teacher." A small tear ran through the pink cheeks of Aarti. Even ghosts cry! Thought Raghu.

May be she was missing her life and the school kids! May be that is the reason she has found Precious trio kids of the same school to listen to her life story.

"Anyway, next day morning father and I started our journey by car. I was unstoppable the whole way. Like a child, I was going on speaking continuously. There were thousands of questions in my mind."

"Will the palace look just like the one seen in pictures and movies? Will the Prince Suraj Singh be dressed up like a king seen in the pictures? Will there be countless number of rooms in the palace? Will there be royal courtroom like the one, which I read in the story books?"

"Keep quiet, dear. Let me concentrate on driving." My father had to scold me to keep me quite for some time.

"With these questions in mind, we arrived at the location of the palace. Prince Suraj Singh, not exactly dressed like king greeted us. He was wearing normal black business suit."

What is business suit?" asked Raghu so casually as if talking to one of his elder sisters. Now the kids started connecting with this little girl who according to them is unfortunate enough to have lost her life so young.

"A business suit is three piece suit normally being worn by business men while meeting important people or making important business deals. Suraj had worn plain white shirt, black coat, black pant and a black tie. Being a young woman, I had a picture in my mind about the prince charming. But, Suraj did not resemble any of the prince-like looks. He was an ordinary person. Perhaps he was born and brought up in London like a normal person, so never got the styles of prince. "Boring looks!!"

"Ohoooo!" The trio said in a single teasing voice. Now they had overcome their fear and started to talk normally with Aarti.

Aarti did not react as she wanted to complete her story before the day ends. More than schoolteachers, she was worried about the kids and really wanted to send them back.

So she continued. "I lost my interests in his looks. Now I got excited for visiting the palace. You will not believe what a palace it was! There were countless number of rooms, big cricket ground size courtroom, corridors four times bigger than our entire building passage. The palace was so vast that we had to take three breaks in between as we were visiting each corner of the palace. It was not a well-maintained place but not so torn out also. We could clearly identify the rooms, kitchen, passages, garden area and a swimming area."

"After visiting the palace for 3 hours, we settled in the garden area in the three chairs kept for us. The servant served three cups of tea and royal imported biscuits to accompany. The cups were uniquely shaped like a mango and printed with beautiful flowers and leaves."

"What I didn't like was the tea as I was fond of milk! That too hot chocolate milk" said Aarti. The kids thought Didi has not grown up at all! And started smiling.

"The prince started the talks. "Sir, did Mam like the palace too?" His tone was very gentle. During the entire visit, he had not behaved like an authority but remained a normal gentleman.

"Lets visit this jungle nearby" my father said. "As I want to build a resort which will be open for public, I need to know the nearby Jungle too. In future if some guests of ours go roaming into the jungle then they should not feel danger."

""Sure". The prince said and led us to this jungle. The palace guard insisted on accompanying us but the prince denied his company."

"We three came to this jungle and after walking for 30 minutes stopped exactly here where you are right now. As you can see the tree above you is the tallest one in this area. We stopped here for some chatting. Suddenly, I saw a human skeleton falling on me.

I got so scared with the accident and having a low BP, I got an immediate heart attack. My father and prince tried to call up a doctor but there was no network in this jungle. After almost struggling to breathe for 10 minutes, I took my last breadth."

"Kids, during my last 10 minutes of life, I had heard something which I could not believe but it was unfortunately true."

"Prince Suraj, I knew it, you will create some mischief here so that I don't buy your palace and run away. I know you have big offers for the property but as you had taken an advance token, you are not able to cancel the deal. So, you planned to scare both of us and cancel the deal. I will not leave you for this." My father was telling to prince. Those were the last words I could hear clearly and left my body but could not leave this world!

Now I am in front of you. I could not go to heaven. I was in search of someone who can help me in taking the revenge with the prince and fulfill my wish. You need to promise me that you will help me in my mission. Anyways you do not have choice. I can let you go right now as your parents and schoolteachers are waiting for you but you will have to come here after 15 days, which will be a Christmas week and help me. Promise me and I will leave you."

The kids promised to help Aarti. Aarti led them to the place where resort staff and school teacher were searching them. At night around 9 p.m. the kids were home.

That night also the kids could not sleep.

The next day morning they planned to meet in the building garden and discuss about how to revisit the resort in next 15 days.

CHAPTER FIVE

The revisit:

Before they could meet in the garden area, they had to answer a hundreds of questions from their parents. Starting from where had you been to what kind of irresponsible children you are, the kids had to answer all of them. Of course, the acts of children of this age was not normal. And now, there is a bigger question that how to revisit the resort? The kids had to anyhow solve this puzzle as they were worried and scared of the Didi.

In the evening, the trio met in the garden.

"I have an idea." said Raghu pointing his forehead with his right hand index finger.

"Let's tell our parents to organize a family picnic in the coming vacation and suggest the same resort to be visited."

"Yes and our parents will jump in the joy of this picnic and immediately agree. Right? Why will they organize the picnic to the same place that we visited just now?" Krina said. Though she was younger to Raghu, she had a better farsightedness than he did.

"Our parents will never take us to the same resort. In fact, I think the elder children picnic which is scheduled in next 15 days to the same resort, also will get cancelled or atleast venue will get changed."

"What? The elder children picnic is scheduled to the same resort and that too in next 15 days?" Asked Lucky.

"Yes. Our neighbor Rohan of class 8 of our school said once." Krina acting just like an adult and matured thinker.

"In that case, we should request our teachers to take three of us along with them in that picnic" said Lucky.

"And you think teachers will agree to this?" asked Raghu who by now realized that they are only children. Who will take children's proposals seriously?

"I think we should atleast ask our teachers. Before asking the question, we should not assume the answers". Said Krina. Now she has turned her side.

So it was decided between the trio to ask the teachers tomorrow about the elder children picnic.

Next day, the trio got ready much before the time and went to school extra fast leaving behind their moms to worry about why children are in so much hurry. Moms nature is always "to worry"!

The trio had decided to speak to Sarika Mam. But, when to speak? The third period was of Sarika Mam. As the teacher entered the classroom, the trio's heartbeat suddenly doubled. The kids had decided to ask the teacher.

"But who will bell the cat?" Krina had a valid question.

"And here, there is no small cat but a real big and elder human being to be belled!" Lucky had supported. Somehow, they are now in the mood of solving the mystery given by Didi rather than studies.

At last after the period got over, there was 30 minutes break. The kids went to staff room. Sarika Mam was busy in preparing some notes for her next class.

Raghu asked very politely, "Mam can we meet today after school for 10 minutes, please?"

Though looking strict for study matters, Sarika Mam was otherwise very friendly with the kids and most worried about them. So, she agreed thinking that kids might have something to share about the resort episode of yesterday. May be their experience in the jungle will help us know better about the resort and will help us in deciding about the upcoming picnic too. The principle Mam had also called the meeting after school to discuss about the picnic venue for elder children.

As the last period got over, the trio immediately reached the staff room to meet Sarika Mam.

"Mam, we want to again visit the resort during the next picnic of elder children. We have to finish some incomplete work over there." Said Krina.

The children are so innocent that they shared the direct matter. No building of plot for putting up the matter in a diplomatic way. Thought Sarika.

"But what is your incomplete work? What were your yesterday's experiences? You know because of your irresponsible act of yesterday, principle Mam is planning to change the picnic venue of bigger kids. Now in such circumstances, you guys want to visit that place again? Aren't you scared of yesterday's experience?" Sarika mam put countless questions in front of the small children.

"Mam, we met one girl yesterday and she had asked us to complete her incomplete work, which is related to resort. She was..." as Raghu was about to speak further, Krina hold his hand signaling not to reveal girl's identity.

Sarika Mam didnt get convinced. She asked "Who is that girl? What is her name?

Raghu said "She is the daughter of Sahani Builders, Ms Aarti."

What Raghu did not say was that the girl was a ghost.

Surprisingly, with this information, Sarika Mam got little bit convinced and allowed the children to join the next picnic.

In the meeting with principle mam that afternoon, she also convinced the entire staff to continue with the venue decision to the same resort for bigger children and requested principal Mam to take the Precious trio children alongwith them explaining her that the children were interested in knowing the various plants and trees in the jungle nearby. Deep inside Sarika mam knew that she is taking a risk but she got ready to do this because of the kids request.

So finally, the trio got the approval to revisit the picnic spot from teachers. But who will now convince their parents? Again, Sarika Mam was contacted and the same reason of children's interest in plants and trees of that jungle was put forward in front of the parents. The parents readily agreed as their children were now portrayed to be more interested in practical studies.

Those were the toughest 15 days for the trio to pass.

"Who knows what will happen? How will Aarti use them in punishing the Prince Suraj? Will she tell the kids to kill him? No, if that is the work to be done, than it will be a strict No. Will she tell them to call the police and get the prince jailed? But, police will ask for the proof. Who will listen to children's stories?" the waves of endless thoughts and questions were roaming like a tornado in the minds of the little kids.

The kids met daily in the garden with all the questions in their minds. But, none of them got resolved.

Finally, the revisit day arrived. This time also kids spent sleepless nights. Not in the excitement and joy but in utmost tensions. They did not bother about packing their swimming suits, games, toys, etc. Their mothers got worried to see this strange behavior but probably kids don't want to go to swimming pool again and might be interested in the plants and trees of the jungle, thought the mothers.

As soon as the trio reached the venue and got orders for playing in swimming pool by teachers, they immediately went straight into the jungle. But, this time all the trees were looking similar.

Which tree was that where they can meet Aarti Didi. So the children started shouting her name and within seconds, the sweet voice got heard.

“Hi kids.” Said Aarti. She was in the same pink and blue clothes, with same ponytail. No change at all.

“Welcome back”. Aarti said as if she is hosting a TV program for the kids. But the kids were not in the funny mood. They only wanted to know what were the expectation of Aarti.

“Didi, please tell us what do you want from us?” Raghu said, as he felt himself the eldest and the most responsible kid of the trio.

“Guys, let me relax you first, else you will remain in tension all the time.” Said Aarti.

“Okay, so let me tell you my plan. You first need to find out where is the prince Suraj right now? Then you need to collect the evidence that he had played a killer trick with me and I died because of that trick. Then you need to call the police and ask them to punish him.”

“This is not so simple Didi.” Said Krina. “Who will give us information about the prince Suraj’s residence? Even if we gather that information, how do we collect the evidence of his trick played on you 9 years back?”

“Good question. I think we can use internet to find out the residence of prince”. Said Lucky.

They immediately searched on their mobile phones and found that the Prince started staying in Mumbai. One of the post also mentioned his current address.

"Fair enough. Lets visit the Prince residence." Lucky said.

"But who will allow the unknown kids to enter the house? His house will have guards and security staff." Said Krina, who is somewhat intelligent in the trio.

"I will give you identity of big elder people and you can enter the residence". Said Aarti.

"How?" the 3 kids asked altogether. Aarti tried to speak some spells on the kids such that they can grow up. But the magic didn't work.

"what you are doing Didi?" Lucky asked.

"I am trying to grow you up by some magic. After all I am a ghost. I can do some magic!"

"But Didi, your magic tricks are not working. Perhaps you are not a seasoned ghost. Forget it." Said Raghu.

"Ghosts are also experts or immature?" asked Aarti making a weird face.

Then suddenly Krina said, "I have an idea. We can dress up and behave like grown up people."

"Great idea". Said Aarti.

"These kids are so innocent, yet so clever." Thought Aarti.

"But we need to do this immediately." Said Lucky, who is always in an exciting mood. No one could meet his energy and ever readiness.

"So tomorrow we will go there" said Lucky.

"But wait we cannot bunk our school. What reason can we give?" Krina said.

"We can go there on Saturday" said Raghu.

"Ok. So it is decided to dress up like big people and visit Prince Suraj on next Saturday." said all three kids unanimously.

Aarti, who was only listening by now, did not get convinced whether these kids will be able to successfully complete the mission or will return empty handed. In any case, she had to agree. She did not have any powers. She could not even move out of this jungle. She was not a "seasoned" Ghost as per the smart kids opinion.

CHAPTER SIX

Visit to Suraj Singh's residence:

The big Saturday arrived. By this time, kids had found the address of Suraj Singh from internet. They could also collect some disguising dresses and material like mustache for boys and long choti for Krina. They had to wear these accessories and some make up on their face. The boys wore ties of their fathers. Krina wore dress of her mother.

But there was one big question! How will they reach to the residence of Suraj? Who will take them?

They remembered of Sarika Mam. They contacted her and asked for her help. Sarika Mam immediately agreed to take them. God knows why Sarika Mam was so much helpful in this matter.

Sarika Mam convinced the parents of the kids for an outdoor tour of Mumbai city for the kids.

Soon, the kids and Sarika Mam reached the residence of the prince. While Sarika Mam stood outside the residence, the kids inquired at the security desk.

"We have to meet Mr. Suraj Singh, as we have an important proposal for him." Said Raghu, always considering him as the most responsible person out of the three kids.

"Do you have an appointment?" asked the guard.

"We don't have appointment but if Suraj will not meet us today, he will loose many things". Said Lucky.

The guard immediately called up Mr. Suraj Singh from the cabin telephone and asked whether the three people can enter the place.

After a while, the guard let them in. This was not a big palace that someone can get lost. This was a small bungalow with hardly 3-4 rooms.

The kids went inside and found the prince. The prince greeted them whole heartedly.

“So tell me. What made you meet me?” the Prince asked, after offering tea and biscuits in royal crockery.

Now, the bigger question in front of kids was how to finish tea? They did not have a habit of drinking tea. So they forgot what brought them here.

Raghu signaled Lucky and Krina to gulp the liquid at once without feeling the taste of it. Later on, they can have the biscuits peacefully.

But, how to drink this at once as it is super hot. Then it was decided to wait until the tea gets cold and then consume it. All these communications happened in sign language.

The prince thought that the big business people are talking among themselves as to how to start the conversation with him.

“Hello, so what is your purpose for visiting me?”

“Oh, yes, we want to buy this property of yours”. Said Raghu, the most responsible one.

“But I don’t want to sell it. I am staying here.” Said Prince.

“Now, what next?” thought three kids. The tea is taking too long to get cold. The biscuits are looking delicious.

Suddenly, Krina started munching the biscuits and the two boys followed the action.

This gave them some comfort and confidence too to speak further.

"We are ready to offer you double price for this place", said Lucky.

"But I still don't want to sell. Where will I stay, if I sell this place?"

"London", all three kids spoke at once.

"No, returning to London is not easy now." Said Prince. He knew that his news kept printed in newspaper and it's a known fact to everyone that he lived in London once upon a time.

"Why don't you want to leave this place? Are you so attached to this place just like you were attached to the palace of your grandfather?" Krina said.

"Yes, I am attached to every place of my ancestor. But how do you know about my grandfather's palace?" asked prince in a shocked voice.

"We know everything about the palace and the story of Builder Sahani and his daughter. The skeleton in the jungle." Said Raghu, now fully confident of his dialogues.

"Ya, it was an accident. Mr. Sahani's daughter had a severe heart attack. There was one skeleton kept by someone which fall down on her and may be she lost her life out of fear." confessed the prince.

"And you had arranged that skeleton." Said Krina.

"Why should I do such mischief? They were my guests. But wait, why should I tell all this to you. You have nothing to do with that story." Said Prince.

"Which was that tree where the skeleton was kept?" asked Krina very smartly.

"It was the tallest tree of the jungle." Said prince.

That's it. The kids were recording all this in their mobile devices. They stopped recording and went away.

Outside the bungalow, they did not meet Sarika Mam but went immediately to police station. Though they narrated entire story to the police, the police did not want to arrest the prince.

"You will get lot of publicity if you arrest the prince. He is not less than a celebrity." Krina used her smartness.

The kids also presented the voice recording and got the police convinced to take the custody of the prince.

The prince was in the lockup now.

Sarika Mam, asked the kids 100 times what happened at the residence of the prince but kids did not answer any of her questions.

Now Sarika Mam had to know desperately what had happened so she revealed why she was taking so much interest in the matter.

"Aarti and me joined our school as teacher, the same day. But her future was in her father's business and she used to accompany her father. This school job was a part time activity for her. Though she was good at teaching, she had to often take leave from school to attend her father's office. One fine day I heard her arguing with principal mam about her often leaves and her student's study getting affected because of this. Sometimes even I had to take her students class as me and her both were teaching Maths. Yet, God knows why students used to like her the most. I was very envious about her popularity among kids.

Deep inside, I knew that she will not remain in school job for a longer time. She will follow her father's business. One day all of a sudden her father came to school to inform the principal Mam that she will not come to school anymore and she got shifted to foreign country to study further on business management. I got all the responsibilities of her students. Though, I did not feel any burden of teaching her students, but the curiosity remained in my mind that how could a person run away overnight. I wanted to know about Aarti and her whereabouts.

That's the reason, I had supported you to know further about Aarti.

The kids revealed the entire truth except the death of Aarti. They did not reveal about the death of Aarti as they knew that if they will say that Aarti's ghost narrated the story of Aarti than Mam will not believe at all.

CHAPTER SEVEN

Mission complete:

Next day, i.e. Sunday, the trio were in a celebration mood now.

They were relaxed that they have solved a big case for a ghost! They met in the garden of the society, their favorite hangout place and discussed about their future in this career.

"Let's open a detective agency. I think we can solve any mystery now." Lucky said with confidence.

"But, do we get enough time from studies for this?" Krina always put logical questions.

"We can take up the cases during vacation." Said Raghu.

"First of all we should name our agency. How about Precious trio?" Suggested Krina.

They unanimously accepted the name at once. That evening, the kids were completely engaged in celebration of their first success and planning for the upcoming agency. The parents were unaware of what was being cooked in their kid's minds.

Meanwhile, in the jungle, Aarti was still waiting for the kid's answer. She did not have any means of communication with kids. She was helpless. One thing she knew that if the prince is punished for his wrongdoing than she will leave this jungle finally. Her desperation increased day by day. But, the celebrating kids were least bothered to inform her.

Five months later,

Today is the first day of summer vacation. Yes, finally kids exams got over, results were out. All the kids were passed and promoted to next class. The kids planned to meet in the garden today evening to discuss on plan for their agency opening now.

Precious Trio Detective Agency

But, look at the newspaper! Suddenly while having breakfast, Raghu read at the backside of the newspaper that his father was reading, there is a small news related to prince. "The Rajwada prince Suraj Singh found innocent in Aarti Sahani case"

Raghu read the full story and it said like this.

"King Vijaysingh's grandson Mr. Suraj Singh, was arrested in December last year for being allegedly involved in Ms. Aarti Sahani, the daughter of Sahani Builder, Murder case. The Sahani Builders had put the allegation that, he had planned a killer prank in the nearby jungle to his ancestor palace during a visit of Builder Sahani and his daughter 10 years back. The builder was inquiring to buy the property and planning to build a big resort in the place of palace. But, the prince had received a better offer from other buyers, therefore he arranged to scare away the builder and his daughter with the help of a skeleton. However, in this small act, Ms. Aarti Sahani lost her life due to heart attack and heart fail.

The further investigations were held and it was found that the prince did not arrange the skeleton. The dead body of the girl is still missing. Thus, the prince was released yesterday, however the police is yet to solve the case that if not prince than who else would do such an act of misguiding the visitors in the jungle."

Raghu immediately took the newspaper and called an urgent meeting in the afternoon instead of evening.

The trio now remembered of meeting Aarti urgently. But how? Will she still be there? If her soul has left the jungle than how will they solve the further mystery? May be this is very strange that 3 live human kids are desperate to meet a dead person and are praying for the meeting!

Here, Ms. Sarika also read the entire story from the newspaper. She was extremely puzzled why kids lied that they met Aarti and Aarti told about the skeleton prank, whereas Aarti is no more! She immediately planned to meet the trio and know the facts and help the kids in solving further mystery.

She called up the kids at once and got completely horrified after knowing that the kids had met the ghost of Aarti in the jungle and the ghost herself told about the skeleton prank!

She couldn't believe this. This time she accompanied the kids to meet Aarti and know if there is anything like ghost.

The trio and Sarika went to the jungle once again. As Sarika was the teacher of the kids, it was not very difficult for her to convince the parents about the kids tour to various places.

The four of them started looking for Aarti. The kids were shouting as if they are calling any school friend of theirs. Sarika was extremely nervous about the things. She also thought once that she shouldn't have come to this jungle but couldn't control her curiosity. Moreover, kids also needed her help to solve the further mystery.

Suddenly, a very soft voice was heard by the kids. "Hi", said Aarti.

"Where were you for so many months? I have been waiting for you. You know I cant even contact you. Did you find Suraj Singh? Did he get arrested?"

Before Aarti could complete her long list of questions, Raghu showed her the newspaper.

Aarti was shocked to know the news.

"Lier! This Suraj Singh must have bribed the officers and got released." Said Aarti.

"Bribed, what is that?" asked Krina. She didn't understand the word.

"To pay a price for an extra undue favour" said Aarti.

Meanwhile Sarika remained at a distance because she didn't want to meet a ghost in any case. She was extremely confused and puzzled and Aarti was so soft spoken that she couldn't listen to the voice of Aarti but shc could listen to the kids. She was so frightened to interrupt the conversation going on with a ghost! With great courage, she went nearer.

"By the way, she is Sarika Mam, Didi" Said Lucky while introducing Sarika Mam to Aarti.

"Oh, yes She and me joined your school together" said Aarti.

Sarika decided to remain as calm as possible. But her shivering hands were uncontrollable. By now she was looking like a horrified cat with big eyes wide open and not able to speak anything in the situation.

"Now you guys don't have any other way to find the truth. Perhaps I will remain in this jungle forever." Said Aarti.

The trio became silent for a moment.

"Whats the conversation going on kids?" after gathering a lot of courage Sarika spoke to the kids.

"Nothing can be done now. Aarti didi is saying Suraj singh must have bribed the officers and got released", said Raghu.

Sarika took the kids to a far tree and started speaking, thinking that ghost will not come here,

"But we need to check the further facts. Lets meet the resort owners here. May be they can tell us from whom they bought the property and constructed the resort."

"Oh Aarti Didi". Said Lucky noticing Aarti nearby only!

And Sarika almost fainted. She somehow gathered the courage as she was the teacher afterall.

"Yes, may be that will help" said Krina.

"Not required" Aarti said. "I know Suraj Singh must have sold this property at a huge price. The greedy man!"

"Now what is greedy man? Aarti didi, you were a maths teacher, how can you use such difficult English words? We cant even google these words! There is no network in our mobiles."

On hearing this, Sarika could not stop her smile.

"Krina, everytime you don't need google. I will tell you the meaning of greedy. It means , it means....."Sarika could not collect the alternate word for greedy.

"It means, wanting more and more", tell this maths teacher, Said Aarti to the kids, teasing Sarika mam. She better remain a maths teacher only" and she blinked her eye.

The kids found it most difficult to hide their laughter.

"Ok, be serious, lets meet the owner of this resort" Said Sarika.

"Yes, we should atleast check once". Said Krina.

The Precious Trio and Sarika mam left for the resort. What a relief was that when Sarika left the jungle! All her shivering looks became normal now. A cold winter was over, she felt.

At the resort, she somehow managed to obtain the appointment of the CEO of the resort whose office was in

Mumbai.

Sarika Mam took the kids to the office of the CEO.

Sarika started conversing with the officer and asked for some agreements of the resort. Now kids were finding all this matter little complicated. They were new to the terms like CEO, price of the resort, agreement, etc. All they could understand was the cup of tea and biscuits kept in front of them! Oh no, not again.

Sarika went through the agreement and explained everything to kids. The trio and Mam drove to the bungalow of Sahani Builders, "Sahani Mensions". On the way, kids made some phone calls.

By the time, they reached the Sahani Mension, they found that Prince Suraj has also reached there. All of them entered at once. There they met the owner of Sahani Builders and Aarti's father. They immediately took him, Suraj and went straight to the jungle near the resort.

This time, they need not call Aarti as she was already waiting for them.

The kids were the intermediaries to converse with the ghost and the living beings as this immature ghost was extra soft spoken!

Nobody had a clue until now what was going on. On one hand everybody except kids were extremely scared of the ghost and other hand, they were not aware of what was going on. Mr. Sahani who was quite upto now, spoke, "can someone tell me what is going on? When prince is found guilty, why are you taking me to this jungle?"

"Because, your daughter is not resting in peace", said Raghu.

"Yes, daddy, I am not in peace". Suddenly Aarti's voice got heard and she was right in front of Mr. Sahani.

Mr. Sahani got frightened now.

"So, will you now tell everything?" said Krina fearlessly.

"Yes, I will tell everything. Actually, Suraj is not guilty. Nine years back, when I read the ad of sale of palace in the newspaper, I wanted to buy the palace anyhow because this location is perfect for a resort, but I knew that the palace would cost much more than my budget. Therefore, I planned to scare Suraj by proving the palace or jungle haunted and take the benefit and bargain with him for a much lower price. My people made the skeleton arrangement in the jungle before our visit to palace.

However, I did not have any idea that the skeleton will scare my daughter and she will have a severe heart attack. I could not accept the truth that the skeleton was arranged by me in front of my half-conscious daughter. I tried to pass on the blame to Suraj. But, unfortunately due to non-availability of any hospital I could not save my daughter from heart attack. Then I tried to seek help from outside this jungle but as I returned back, my daughter was missing. I found her scarf totally wet with her blood. It was the act of a wild animal. I also filed her missing complaint with police, but deep inside I knew that she is no more.

After this event, I was totally broken. But as elders say, the show must go on. I had to run the business anyhow. There are thousands of employees working in my company. So sitting with a broken heart will not help. Somehow, I returned back to the business. I got the benefit of lower price of the palace and built this resort, because Suraj was in need to sell the palace at any cost. But, I got the fruits of my bad deeds. I wanted to harm Suraj, but harmed my self and my family in return. The resort which I built was supposed to be managed by my daughter Aarti, but she is not there anymore"

"No papa, you cant do this." Said Aarti. "I thought that Suraj would have scared you with the concept of haunted jungle but you being my brave papa, have still gone ahead and bought the palace and built this resort! I always wanted to talk to someone who can believe that I was dead and I wanted justice for me and my father. But I never knew that you are the original criminal"

"Papa, you had arranged that skeleton?"

"How can you do this Papa? I never thought money becomes so important for a person that he can indulge into any unfair means of saving or making money!! I am so glad that I remained here and didn't live with you."

"Mr. Suraj, I am extremely sorry, that I had a wrong perception about you and told these kids to get you arrested. I think now my mission is complete and I will rest in peace." And those were the last words of Ms. Aarti.

She went deep into the jungle. The kids tried to call her but there was no reply.

Immediately there appeared police as per the phone call of kids and Mr. Sahani was arrested. Everything was now settled. But, the kids still wanted to meet Aarti once if possible.

CHAPTER EIGHT

The search of Aarti!

The kids went in the direction where Aarti had gone. After walking only a kilometer, they met Aarti once again. Oh my god! She was having food! Do Ghost eat like human beings?

Aarti got surprised that kids are so brave that they followed her.

"What is this Didi? We solved your murder mystery and you are not murdered at all?"

"You lied to us? Did you try to scare us? Why, such a drama of being a ghost? And what about the dead body that you told is buried under that tallest tree?" Aarti could not make out which kid was asking which question. But all these questions were showered on her like stormy rains by all the three kids.

Now its Aarti's turn to reveal the truth about her.

"Here is Aarti, a very helpless but brave girl in front of you."

"Yes, I got heart attack after seeing skeleton, but I did not die. My father and Prince Suraj went to seek help leaving me unconscious here. After 3 hours, I got conscious and found myself with these simple villagers. They told me that a tiger was trying to carry me with him. So, they fought with the tiger and saved me and brought me to this village."

"Why didn't you return to your house?" Asked Raghu.

"How to return? I was bedridden for 3 months. After that I lost my way to palace. I was in constant wait of someone who can help me. More then finding my way, I wanted to punish Prince Suraj Singh thinking that he tried to kill me. So, I waited here for right help. And you were the right help sent by God. When I said I am dead, I wanted to scare you so that you take me seriously. I was really helpless that time."

"What about these villagers?" asked krina.

"They had already saved my life. I didn't want to trouble them more. On the contrary I am helping them in their work."

"Will you return to your house now? Your father's business and the resort need you." This time it was Lucky.

Suddenly after solving this case, the kids had got more intelligence.

"Yes, I will return to my house and manage this resort."

Now the kids had real celebration time. All this time they thought that they have solved a case for a ghost, so they were scared of asking the fees from a ghost.

But this is Sahani Builder's daughter right in front of them. They can demand any fees that they want.

Ms. Aarti Sahani is managing the resort now. She had ordered the management of resort to provide best of the services to all the guests and listen to all the suggestions of the visitors. Special discounts to school picnics!!

Thanks to the Precious trio.

"Mam, can you explain, what was written in the agreement?" asked Raghu sitting among the interviewers panel to Sarika Mam.

"On reading the entire agreement, I found that the palace was bought at a much lower price than the market price that too by Sahani Builders! So I thought if Suraj was the actual criminal, then why Mr. Sahani would still buy the property from the murderer of his daughter?"

"The interview is over, we will let you know whether you are selected or not" said Krina.

The Precious trio is now thinking of taking Sarika Mam as their assistant agent and she will be in charge of analyzing various documents and agreements like a grown up person in their upcoming agency named "The Precious trio".

The three small school going kids going for a school picnic, got into a situation where they are forced to solve a mystery. Check out how they find the solution initially because of the force but later they plan to open their own detective agency.

Thanks for reading the book. Hope you enjoyed the book. Upcoming are more and more such mystery cases to be solved by the Precious Trio agency.

Printed by Libri Plureos GmbH in Hamburg, Germany